Love at Last

A
Braden
Flirt

Love in Bloom Series

Melissa Foster

ISBN-10: 1-948004-82-8
ISBN-13: 978-1-948004-82-4

LOVE AT LAST

Cover Design: Elizabeth Mackey Designs
Cover Photograph: Sara Eirew

WORLD LITERARY PRESS
PRINTED IN THE UNITED STATES OF AMERICA

A Note from Melissa

If this is your first introduction to the Bradens, please note that this is a *flirt* not a full-length novel. *Love at Last* follows Cal Hayden and Rachel Gray, friends of the Bradens, and also features several of the Colorado Bradens. *Love at Last* is a great way to get to know the Braden family, and then you can go back and read each of their love stories. Like all Love in Bloom books, flirts are written to stand alone, so jump right in and enjoy the fun, sexy, and emotional ride.

What is a Flirt?

The Love in Bloom big-family romance world has become so widely enjoyed, I have been asked by thousands of readers to write the stories of our beloved side characters. While I couldn't possibly fit in writing full-length novels for each of them while maintaining my normal publication schedule, I've created *flirts*. Flirts vary in length, and cover twenty-four to forty-eight hours of two side characters' lives on their path to their happily ever after, while also updating readers about their favorite main characters. I hope you love these quick, fun, sexy stories as much as I enjoy writing them.

If this is your first Love in Bloom story, then you have a whole series of loyal, sexy, and wickedly naughty heroes and smart, sassy heroines to catch up with. The characters from each family series within the Love in Bloom world cross into other family series and make appearances in future books so you never miss an engagement, wedding, or birth.

Start reading the Love in Bloom big-family romance collection FREE with *Sisters in Love*, the story that started the sensation, the very first of the Love in Bloom books. www.Melissafoster.com/LIBFree

Visit my website for family trees, reading order, and publication schedules.
www.melissafoster.com/reader-goodies

Sign up for my newsletter to keep up to date with new releases, sales, and events.
www.melissafoster.com/newsletter

Thanks for reading!

Melissa

Chapter One

"THREE GIRLS WALK into a diner. One's recently married and the happiest she's ever been, one's pregnant and ready to pop, and one's lusting after a man who has no clue she fantasizes about his big—"

"Stop!" Rachel Gray slapped her hand over her friend Emily's mouth as they neared the town diner. Emily had recently returned from Italy, where she'd married her long-time fiancé, Dae Bray, and her sister-in-law Callie was eight and a half months pregnant. They were two of Rachel's closest friends and they were living their dreams, while Rachel crushed on a man who had been flirting shamelessly with her, toying with her emotions. It was so different from the gentleman she knew him to be, it made for a roller coaster of emotions every time she saw him. The fact that he'd never asked her out only amped up her frustration, which was why she'd made up her mind the last time she'd seen him that she was *done* letting Cal Hayden get under her skin.

Or at least she was trying to be done.

"Do *not* go there," she said to Emily. "And for Pete's sake, please don't say a word about that in front of Margie."

Margie Holmes had worked at the diner *forever.* She was the eyes and ears of Trusty, Colorado, their quaint hometown, and Rachel would like to stay out of her gossip web, *thank you very much.*

"If you think Margie's gossip tentacles don't stretch far and wide, you are wrong." Callie patted her burgeoning belly and said, "Margie knew I was pregnant before Wes and I did."

Rachel laughed as she opened the door for the girls to pass through. Today was the Trusty Spring Festival, one of the biggest events of the year. Most of the shops had closed for the event, including Rachel's hair salon, but the diner remained open. Residents liked to joke that it was Margie's way of keeping tabs on them.

"Hot cowboy alert," Emily whispered as she passed through.

Rachel followed them in and stopped cold at the sight of the most perfect Levi's-clad butt she'd ever seen. She'd know that sculpted perfection anywhere. Heat chased up her spine as she took in the strong lines of Cal Hayden's trim waist and the way the soft white cotton stretched across his broad shoulders and back as he leaned over the counter chatting with Margie. Cal was one of the most sought-after horse trainers in the area, and he was six-plus feet of pure Rachel-wrecking virility.

He turned and, *sweet baby Jesus*, his black Stetson shaded his cerulean-blue eyes, which reached right into her chest and stroked her heart. Yes, her *heart*, because despite his flirting-on-steroids nonsense of late, he was the epitome of a gentleman. There were lots of hot guys around, cowboys even, but single gentlemen who looked beyond a woman's figure, who knew the importance of family, and who could dance like Fred Astaire? Not in her small hometown. Cal was one in a million.

He leaned to the side, revealing Li'l Hal Braden sitting on the counter, safely nestled in the circle of his arm, and she melted right there on the spot. Li'l Hal was just shy of a year and a half, with a mop of dark hair like his parents, Emily's cousin Rex and Rex's wife, Jade. Yes, Li'l Hal was cuter than a litter of kittens, and seeing all that cuteness wrapped up in Cal's hotness sent Rachel's hormones into overdrive.

So much for resisting Cal Hayden.

"Hey there, darlin'," he said with a rich drawl as a slow smile spread across his too-handsome face. "You going to come in and join us, or stare at my butt all day long?"

"I was looking at the baby," she protested as she stepped inside.

"Yeah, the *baby*," Emily mumbled.

"Mm-hm, it's all about the baby," Callie said with a

laugh.

"How's it going, girls?" Margie asked from behind the counter. "Go ahead and take a seat. I'll be right over." She winked at Rachel and said, "You might want the booth by the window. Great view of the counter from there."

Ohmygod.

Cal's lips tipped up in a cocky smile. Rachel tried to keep from blushing, but she could feel her cheeks burning.

"I've got it. I want to get off my feet anyway." Callie went to claim the booth.

"Look at what you started," Rachel whispered sharply to Cal as Emily reached for Li'l Hal.

He leaned in and spoke in a husky voice, just loud enough for her ears only. "Did you like what you saw? Because I sure do." His eyes darkened, and he added, "Be sure to save me a dance at the festival, darlin'."

Her stomach somersaulted.

Before she could respond, Emily asked, "Why do you have my adorable nephew?" She bounced the little one on her hip, earning sweet baby giggles.

Cal rose to his full height, bringing every delicious inch of him into focus. "Rex is at the festival, and Jade's morning sickness was bad this morning. I offered to watch him for a few hours."

"Did you hear that, Rachel?" Emily said sassily. "Cal likes babies."

Rachel rolled her eyes, opening her mouth to deny that she cared, but Cal was watching her like a hawk, and her ability to respond flitted away. Oh, how she hated that! She was *not* a mousy girl who withered at the sight of a hot man! *Just a woman who had fallen so hard for one it bordered on ridiculous.*

"I like things that come in small packages," Cal said with a lift of his brow.

The door to the diner opened, and the brisk air snapped Rachel's lust-addled brain into gear again. *Okay, big boy, that was a direct hit.* Rachel was barely five feet tall. It was time for that cowboy to ride or get out of the stable.

"Funny, I prefer *big* packages," she said with enough snark to cause the man sitting at the other end of the counter to mumble, "Damn."

Cal's eyes smoldered, and she felt the heat follow her all the way to the booth. She sat across from Callie, her back to Cal, and whispered, "I can't believe I said that!"

Callie tucked her dark hair behind her ear and said, "I can't believe you two are still dancing around each other."

Rachel turned and stole a glance at Emily, who was handing the baby back to Cal. Heck if seeing that baby snuggled up against him didn't send her insides into another wild flurry. She turned around and inhaled deeply, needing a distraction. "So, Wes is riding in the rodeo at the festival? Are you excited to watch him?"

"Yes, but even after all this time it still makes me nervous." Callie hadn't even ridden a horse before meeting Wes, and while he was a thrill seeker, she was a demure librarian who preferred fairy tales to danger.

Emily slid into the booth beside Callie, and half a second later, Cal placed a high chair at the table catty-corner from them and settled Li'l Hal into it. Rachel had just started to calm down, and his close proximity made her pulse kick up again. She tried not to watch him, but as he pressed a kiss to the top of Li'l Hal's head, his eyes connected with hers and he winked.

Could this get any more embarrassing? The guy was leading her on, and she was hanging on to his every breath. She needed to get a grip, and this time she *meant* it. She was going to forget about him if it was the last thing she did. Clearing her throat, she forced herself to focus on her friends instead of the beefcake who was currently reading the menu to a baby.

Good Lord.

Thankfully, Margie appeared to take their order. "Okay, what can I get y'all? The usual?"

"Yes," they said in unison—though Rachel thought, *I'll take one hot cowboy with a side of baby.*

"Coming right up," Margie said, and moved to take Cal's order.

Do not look at him.

"I brought the wedding pictures." Emily pulled a wedding album from her purse and set it on the table between them.

Do not listen for his order. Rachel's eyes skimmed the gorgeous pictures of Emily and Dae.

"It was chilly, but that's better than hot, right?" Emily said as she turned the page, describing every detail of her wedding.

Rachel hadn't been able to travel to Italy for the wedding, and she wanted to hear about it, but even as she kept her eyes on the pictures, she couldn't register a word Emily said. She was too busy trying not to concentrate on Cal.

"I'll take a big piece of blondie pie, with extra whipped cream," Cal said.

Rachel's gaze snapped to his. He was staring right at her with a smile that made her insides go crazy.

"You do realize it's breakfast time?" Margie asked.

Without looking away, Cal said, "I could eat it morning, noon, and night."

Holy moly.

Rachel's cell phone rang, startling her out of her reverie. She fumbled in her purse, silently chastising herself for getting lost in Cal again, and stared out the window as she answered the call from Emily's cousin's wife. "Hi, Max."

"Hi. Are you around?" Max asked frantically. "I know you're not working today, but Dylan just cut off one of

Adriana's ponytails, and we have family photos next week. I only turned my back for a second to wipe Bryce's nose, and Dylan had those little kid scissors. The ones with the rounded tips. I didn't even know they could cut hair." Bryce was Max's newest baby.

"It happens all the time," Rachel assured her. "Don't worry. I'll fix her right up and she'll be cute as a button. I'm at the diner. Can you meet me at my shop in ten minutes?"

After she ended the call, she pushed to her feet. "I've got to run."

"What's wrong?" Emily asked.

"Dylan cut off one of Adriana's ponytails." Not that Rachel was happy about Adriana's plight, but selfishly, she was glad for the excuse to leave. If she looked at Cal Hayden one more time, she was likely to go up in flames.

Callie and Emily gasped.

"Max must be so upset," Callie said. "She loved Adriana's long hair."

"That little *rascal*," Emily said. "I can't believe he did that."

"It's more common than you think. I better run. I'll catch up with you at the festival." She put a few dollars on the table and ran out the door.

LATER THAT AFTERNOON, Cal stood outside the arena and scanned the festival grounds for the hundredth time since he'd arrived, hoping to catch sight of Rachel.

"Hey there," a stacked brunette said with a flirtatious wave.

Cal nodded and turned back to the mare he was grooming. He was riding one of Luke Braden's horses for a show soon, and couldn't escape the barn. Unfortunately, these events brought out every cowboy-seeking woman there was from all the surrounding towns. The place had been mobbed—and he'd been hit on—all freaking day. As much as he loved these events, and he really did love community events, he could do without the women wasting his time with stupid comments like *I bet you're great at riding bareback.* They thought they were irresistible in their cleavage-baring shirts, and clever with their double entendres, but Cal only had eyes for one green-eyed girl, and she didn't have to rely on tricks to get his attention. She'd had it for years, and he was finally in a position to make his move. If only he knew where she was.

He saw Luke approaching from the far side of the barn with his brothers Jake and Pierce. They were a formidable force, the three brawny Braden men. *Solid country stock,* as his father would have said, rest his soul. They'd grown up in Trusty, whereas Cal had grown up just outside the city limits. But the horse community was closely knit, and he'd known the Bradens for years.

"How're my beautiful girls?" Luke asked as he joined Cal by the stall of one of his horses. Luke was the best gypsy horse breeder in the States. Gypsy horses were stunning creatures, with silky manes and tails and feathering that covered their hooves. They were a needy breed in general, and Luke had showered each of his horses with love, which they gave back in droves, as the horse was doing now, pressing her head into the center of his chest.

"They're ready and waiting." Cal extended a hand to Pierce, who owned resorts all over the world and lived in Reno. "Haven't seen you in months. I hear congratulations are in order."

Pierce took his hand and pulled him into a manly embrace. "On the wedding or the pregnancy?" He and his wife, Rebecca, had eloped a few months ago, and word around town was that Rebecca had gotten pregnant on their wedding night.

"That'd be both," Cal said, and turned to Jake, who worked as a stuntman and lived in Los Angeles with his wife, Fiona. They came back for the festival every year. "Hey, man. Good to see you."

"How's it going?" Jake embraced him. "Sorry to hear about your old man."

Even after six months, the realization that his father was really gone still stung. He'd battled cancer for almost two years, and not a day passed when Cal didn't miss him. "Thank you."

"How's your mom holding up?" Jake asked.

"She's good. Thanks for asking. She's around here somewhere, hanging out with the women from her book club."

"Good," Jake said. "It's nice that she's got close friends. You haven't seen my wife around, have you? She took off with Emily and a few of the girls and I haven't seen her since."

"Fiona?" Cal shook his head. "No, but there are so many people here, I could have just missed her. Was Rachel Gray with them by any chance?" When she'd run out of the diner, Emily had told him she'd had a *hair emergency* to take care of, whatever that was. He'd been *this close* to bringing her breakfast to the salon when Emily mentioned she was heading over with it. Now it was nearing six o'clock and he had yet to set his eyes on her.

"Rachel? Yeah, she was with them," Jake said. "She told me about Dylan cutting Adriana's hair."

"That must be the hair emergency Emily mentioned."

"Oh yes. Adriana's now sporting a pixie cut, at least that's what Rachel called it." Jake laughed and said, "But Dylan? That boy's gonna get into some shit when he's older."

"Reminds me of someone else I know," Pierce said with a smirk.

"Proud of it," Jake said, and smacked Cal on the back.

"What's up with you and Rachel?"

"Not enough," Cal said. "But I'm fixin' to change that if I can find her."

"*After* our show, please," Luke said, tapping his watch.

They spent a few more minutes catching up, and then Cal and Luke saddled up and rode two of Luke's finest horses into the ring. Cal handled all types of horse training, and he'd helped Luke with trick training his *girls*. As they trotted out to the center and got into position with the horses facing each other, Cal did another quick visual sweep of the area and spotted his blond beauty watching from the far side of the ring. He sat up taller and lifted his chin in her direction, but she turned at that very moment to Cutter Long, one of Wes's employees at his dude ranch. Cutter was a nice guy, but the idea of the dark-haired cowboy hitting on Rachel made his blood boil.

It took all his focus to work through the performance and not head straight out of the ring, swoop Rachel off her feet, and ride away with her.

The horses performed gracefully, easily handling the side passes, marches, and a host of other tricks as they mirrored each other's actions. Cal knew how important it was to remain at ease when he was on any horse. They were sensitive creatures, and Luke's horses had worked too hard to be thrown off their game because of his jealousy. But hell if reining in his emotions wasn't like trying to tame a wild bull.

He tried to focus on the show, refusing himself even a glance at Rachel.

By the time the show came to an end and the horses bowed, earning loud cheers from the crowd, Cal was about at his wit's end.

As he rode out of the ring, he chanced a look in the direction where Rachel had been—and felt gutted that both she and Cutter were gone.

Chapter Two

AFTER GETTING THE horses settled, Cal went in search of Rachel, walking in the direction of where he'd seen her earlier. The crowd was dispersing, and he was walking against the flow. People congratulated him on the show, and friends stopped to chat, but Cal was too focused on finding Rachel to want to waste any time. He politely tipped his hat, moving away as quickly as he could without being rude. There was a break before the rodeo began, and he had hoped to spend that time with Rachel.

Goddamn it. He should have made his move at the diner instead of bullshit flirting. He didn't like the desperate switch that had flipped in his head. He'd felt her pulling away, and that had catapulted him into someone he wasn't.

I should have made my move ages ago.

He climbed up on the fence to get a better look and spotted Rachel standing with Cutter on the other side of the ring. Her back was to Cal, but he'd know her anywhere. He hopped over the fence and jogged across the ring. Every determined step brought a huff of arrogance. He'd be damned if he was going to lose her to *any* other man. He put one hand on the top of the fence and propelled himself over it, landing behind them with a *thud*.

Rachel and Cutter turned, and that slightly shy, megawatt smile he adored appeared on her face, soothing the ire that had mounted inside him. Her long blond hair hung in gentle waves over her shoulders. The chocolate-brown sweater she wore had one of those drapey necklines, and the sleeves hung over the lower part of her hands. There was nothing curve-hugging about it. Her jeans were tight, but the sweater hung almost to her thighs. And still, with her knee-high brown suede boots and those bedroom eyes, she was the sexiest woman he'd ever seen, and he was determined to make her *his*.

"Hey," she said a little breathlessly. "That was an amazing show."

"Thanks, beautiful." He didn't hesitate as he draped an arm over her shoulder and said, "Hey, Cutter. Thanks for keeping Rachel company, but I've got something I need to show her."

Confusion rose in both Rachel's and Cutter's eyes.

"I…uh…no problem," Cutter said.

"Great. We'll catch ya later." Cal guided Rachel away.

She blinked her pale green, curious eyes up at him.

"Where are we going?"

"Like I said, I want to show you something." He headed for the craft tent across the field, telling himself not to ask if she was into Cutter. It was killing him not knowing, but it didn't matter if she was. He'd win her over come hell or high water.

"Okay," she said skeptically, looking over her shoulder in the direction Cutter had gone. "But that was kind of rude."

She was right, and being rude or lying went against everything he'd been taught and the way he lived his life. He couldn't fix the rude part, and he wasn't about to lie to Rachel, so he went with, "Yeah, probably."

She looked up at him with wide eyes. "Cal, *what* is going on? Do you have a problem with Cutter?"

"Nope," he said as they weaved around a group of people eating ice-cream cones.

"Sure seemed like you did."

He looked down at her and his stomach went all squirrely. "I've got a problem with Cutter hitting on you."

"What?" she asked with a laugh. "Why?"

"Because it's my turn to hit on you."

"Wait, what? Your *turn*? You flirt with me all the time."

He stopped walking and gazed into her confused eyes. "Flirting with you and hitting on you are two different things."

She crossed her arms, the confusion morphing to amusement. "Enlighten me, wise flirtatious one."

He chuckled. "Flirting is something you do when you're feeling out the situation. Getting a read on each other's emotions." He stepped closer, touched his fingers to hers, and enjoyed the slight hitch to her breathing. He lowered his voice so she had to listen carefully and would hear every word he said. "And hitting on someone is something you do when you know they're the one you want to take home that night."

Her brows knitted. "So, you think you're going to have *sex* with me tonight? After you've toyed with me for months? Well, I've got news for you, Cal Hayden. I'm *not* that type of girl."

"Relax. I know you're not. Having sex is not on my agenda." Although *making love* to Rachel was definitely on his mind. He took her hand and continued walking toward the craft tent. "Come on, darlin'. We have candles to make."

"Candles? What has gotten into you?" She smiled as they followed a group of people into the craft area.

Tables lined the walls of the tent offering all sorts of do-it-yourself crafts, like wreath making, string art, pottery, and about a dozen other options. It smelled like wax and cinnamon. Children laughed as they darted around the tables, and he could hear smiles in the din of the crowd.

"What *is* on your agenda tonight?" Rachel asked.

He leaned down and said, "Only you, darlin'," and then he handed a twenty-dollar bill to the woman behind the candlemaking table. "We'd like to make four candles, please."

The woman handed them four tickets and a basket, then pointed to another table, where they were directed to choose four glass jars.

"What if I have plans?" Rachel asked.

He hadn't thought of that and realized his mistake. "Then that would make me rude for not checking. My apologies. Do you have plans?"

"Well, no, but…" Her lips curved up in another sweet smile. "I could have."

"You're right. I shouldn't have assumed. Rachel, will you allow me to monopolize the next few hours?"

"The next few *hours*?" She pressed her lips together, looking sweet and sexy with her brows knitted tightly and her unstoppable smile peeking out despite her efforts to hide it.

RACHEL LOOKED AROUND the tent wondering what alternate universe she'd stepped into to have Cal Hayden pursuing her so purposefully, much less wanting to make *candles*. When she was watching him ride the horse, all she could think about was how capable and confident he was, and how she wanted to be a lot more than someone he toyed with. And when Cutter came over, she tried to turn off her feelings for Cal. After all, Cal hadn't seemed to want to do more than flirt with her. But turning off her emotions wasn't an option. Heck, flirting with another guy wasn't even an option. Poor Cutter was met with uncaring responses like *uh-huh* and *that's nice*. She'd moved to the other end of the ring, hoping to shake him, but Cutter had followed her over.

She gazed up at the frustratingly handsome object of her affection and wondered what this was to him. A game? A challenge? The warmth and *hope* in his eyes told her it was neither, and that both thrilled her and made her nervous.

"Okay," she said shakily. "But I'm not going to sleep with you. I don't even know what to make of all this."

He squeezed her hand, a relieved smile curving his lips. "Trust me, sweetheart. By the end of tonight, you'll know exactly what to make of *us*."

Oh boy. Us? Was he saying what she thought? What she'd hoped for too long to believe?

They chose four jars and put them in the basket. Then they moved on to the next table, to choose the scents for their candles. There must have been thirty or more to choose from, which was a little overwhelming, made even more so by every brush of Cal's leg, hip, or shoulder against her. She was *too* aware of his every move, and his every glance. There could be a thousand fragrances, but all she smelled was one particular rugged cowboy.

"Vanilla?" she suggested.

"That'll make you hungry." He waggled his brows and

snagged the fragrance jar from her hands. "We'll take it."

She laughed and picked up another. "Sandalwood?"

He arched a brow, a playful smile tugging at his lips. "Anything that inspires wood has to be good, right?"

"Cal!" Laughter fell from her lips.

"Don't worry, darlin'. I don't need a candle when I've got you by my side."

"Ohmygosh." She felt herself blushing. "I don't even know who you are right now."

He put his mouth beside her ear and said, "I'm the guy who knows what he wants, remember?"

Her heart did a happy dance, and she was too breathless to respond.

"How about this? Pure Innocence?" He wiggled the fragrance jar. "That's you personified. And now it's *mine*."

The redhead behind the scent table held up a fragrance jar and said, "We have the perfect scent for young lovers."

"Oh," Rachel said, "we're not—"

"*That young*," Cal said, reaching for the jar with a cocky grin. He smelled it and held it out for Rachel to do the same.

She sniffed the musky, sweet scent. "Oh, that's nice."

"It's called Satin Sheets," he said. "We're taking this one, too."

"I thought you said sex wasn't on your agenda," she whispered.

"It's not." He put his arm around her and led her to the

next table. "But maybe it's on *yours*."

"Mine?"

"I see the way you look at me."

She was about to deny it, but he cocked his head with a challenge in his eyes, and they both laughed.

"Okay, maybe you're not so bad to look at," she said as they sat at a picnic table to make their candles.

One of the women who was running the station came over and explained the candlemaking process.

"Measure, melt, wick, fragrance, pour. I think we can handle this." Cal bumped Rachel's shoulder. "Right, lover?"

She laughed. "Yeah. Right."

"Okay, then. If you need me, just holler." The woman moved to the next table to help another couple.

"Lover?" Rachel asked.

"Like I said, I see that hope in your eyes."

But could he see the bigger hope in her heart, which was holding tight to each of his comments, wishing for more than a sexy night?

They worked together to measure the wax for each candle and melt it.

"We're supposed to dip the little silver base of the wick into the wax and stick it to the bottom of the jars," she reminded him.

"I usually don't let women play with my wick on the first date, but…" His gaze heated.

Lust simmered inside her, and she felt her cheeks heat up *again*. "Are you *trying* to make me blush?"

He shrugged. "You're the one who wants my wick. I'm trying to behave, but you've got one hand on my thigh." He picked up her hand and placed it on his thigh. "And you're looking at me like I'm a piece of meat. I mean, it's a little hard to miss the fact that you're sizing me up."

She laughed. "You're *so* cute, it's ridiculous."

"Cute?" He leaned closer and said, "Or *hot?*"

Their eyes connected, and her heart did a fluttery thing, which felt an awful lot like what happened in those pre-kiss seconds, when her skin would sizzle and her eyelids would grow heavy. It had been ages since she'd kissed a man, and Cal wasn't leaning in. *Which means I'm in this moment alone.*

Oh crud!

"*Wicks,*" fell from her lips. She scrambled for a wick and dipped the little metal base on the bottom of the wick into the melted wax. Then, with shaky hands, she lowered it into the jar.

"Here." He secured a clothespin on the top of the wick and balanced it on the rim of the jar. "You don't want that to fall in."

"How do you know so much about candlemaking?"

"If I told you, I'd have to kill you."

He smiled, and it wasn't the flirtatious one that she'd seen so often lately. It was his genuine, warm smile. The one that had captured her attention when he'd walked into the diner a few years ago while she was eating breakfast. First she'd seen his smile and then she'd seen his butt. She'd been unable to look away from either ever since.

They fell silently into sync, adding the wicks to the other jars and securing them with clothespins. Cal moved the pot in which the wax had melted to the cooling tray and turned to face Rachel with a serious expression.

"We have to talk about something," he said, and she leaned closer so as not to miss a word. "How do you feel about satin sheets?"

It took her a second to figure out if he was talking about the fragrance or not, and she decided to jump in on his little game. "I like satin sheets very much, as long as there's a little sweetness between them." She picked up the vanilla fragrance jar and wiggled it.

"Hm." He narrowed his eyes seductively. "Are you opposed to a little heat between the sheets, or do you prefer *pure innocence*?"

She felt her cheeks burning and forced herself to hold his gaze. "How can you stoke a fire if you don't heat up the wood?" She reached for the sandalwood bottle, feeling bold and naughty, and placed it in his hand.

His fingers curled around hers, and he looked at her like nothing else existed. Electricity zinged inside her like a pinball. This was the moment she'd dreamed about, the one she'd tried to give up on only a few hours ago. Her heart told her to go with it, to lean in and take the kiss she'd been dying for. But she couldn't ignore the red flags waving in her head. She knew Cal wasn't a player. That wasn't what was worrying her. There was never any gossip about him and other women. He hadn't even buried his grief in alcohol or women when he'd lost his father. Rachel had wanted to be there for him then, but he'd been surrounded by his guy friends. That was what he'd seemed to need at the time, regardless of how she'd ached for him. But was this real, or a figment of her hopes and dreams? He'd said all the right things, but she'd wanted him for so long she needed clarity before they kissed even once. One taste would never be enough.

She nervously withdrew her hand from his and reached for the handle of the pot. Cal put his hand over hers, rough, warm, and so big, it swallowed hers up.

"Be careful, darlin'. I don't want my girl getting burned."

She sighed, reveling in his endearment.

They lifted the pot together and poured the wax into the jars.

"I thought I knew you," she finally said, "but I'm beginning to think you're two different people."

"That might be fun." He waggled his brows again.

"I'm serious. You're the epitome of a gentleman most of the time, and then you started shamelessly flirting with me, but you've never asked me out. And now you're acting like we've been a couple forever. I don't want to play games, Cal. I can't keep up."

"I don't want to play games either."

One of the women who worked there brought over a metal tray. "You two did a great job! I'll put these in the cooling area, and you can come get them in a few hours. Do you still have your tickets?"

"We do, thank you," Cal said as Rachel rose to her feet. His gaze warmed again as he took her hand. "Ready?"

They left the bright lights of the tent, and she said, "You never answered my question. If you really like me and this isn't some sort of…I don't know what, then why haven't you asked me out?"

The dusky night air sent a chill through her, or that might have been her nerves, because they stopped beneath a big, beautiful tree, which had been decorated with tiny white lights, and when Cal faced her, the emotions in his eyes were palpable.

"You don't just go up to the prettiest horse in the stable and climb on board, Rachel. First you have to spend time with her, get to know what settles her, what makes her jumpy. Learn what makes pride shimmer in her eyes. You need to earn her trust and be fully committed, ready to take on such an important responsibility. That type of trust doesn't come easily, and it needs to be so real that when you look into her eyes, there's no doubt lingering there."

He brushed a lock of her hair from her cheek and cupped her face with his warm hand. Between the intimate touch and the way he was gazing into her eyes, she could barely breathe.

"Over the past few years, I've learned that you're not the type of girl who flaunts herself with the need to be the center of attention. You like to blend in, to be noticed for who you are, not for your incredible beauty. You're soft, but not naively innocent, and strong, which shows in how you carry yourself and the way you run your business. You're creative, making those little signs you set around town, and you're generous to a fault—giving those signs to people to brighten their days."

Holy cow, he knew about her signs? She'd started painting old pieces of wood her father had lying around when she was young. She'd paint friendly or inspirational phrases because they made her happy, and her parents always hung them up in the house, the barn, the porch. One day when a neighbor had gotten ill, she'd made one for him, and when she saw the joy it had given him, she'd begun making them for other friends, people who were going through hard times.

"Do you know why I put them around town?" she asked. "Or leave them on park benches?"

"I have a theory," he said evenly. "I think you like to see people smile."

She nodded. "It's silly. Simple, really, but I think kindness matters a lot more than people give it credit for."

"Everything about you matters, darlin', and your big heart is only one of the reasons you've captured mine."

Oh boy…this is definitely happening.

She swallowed against the adrenaline filling her up inside.

"Rachel, you're sweet and funny, but I think you have a bit of temptress in you that makes you blush. I know you like to dance, but not wild and dirty like some girls do. You prefer slow dancing, and when you dance fast, as I've seen you do at weddings and events like these, you're totally focused on the people or person you're dancing with, not on who else might be looking at you."

She felt like she was suddenly seeing the *real* Cal. The man who, a year ago, she didn't think even knew she existed. But he had noticed her, and he was pouring out his heart and soul, trusting her with his honesty.

"I didn't think you'd noticed me much at all until you started flirting with me."

"I'd have to be blind not to notice you, darlin'. You outshine every other woman in this town."

She lowered her gaze as heat rushed up her chest. He lifted her chin with his hand and slid it to the nape of her neck, stepping closer. She was breathing so hard, and he was so close, her breasts brushed against his abdomen.

"You're an observer," he said softly. "I'm surprised you didn't notice."

"I…" She shook her head, trying to pinpoint when the

flirtatious Cal had appeared, but all of him ran together in her mind. "Before you started all the flirting stuff, you were such a gentleman, I had no idea you were into me."

His lips curved up in a smile that reached his eyes. "My father would have appreciated knowing that. It's a testament to how my parents raised me. I wasn't raised to be the kind of man who flirts the way I have been with you."

"Then why have you been doing it? Not that I mind," she said quickly, "but I'm curious because it was so out of character it threw me off-kilter."

His eyes darkened, and he stepped impossibly closer. "Because I got a little lost, or maybe *desperate* is a better word. I felt something changing in you, like you were losing faith in me. I know that's ridiculous, because you weren't mine to start with, but I was building up to asking you out, Rachel, and I had a feeling you were building up to something, too."

Oh God, you saw that?

She thought he hadn't even noticed her, and she had been ready to give up on him—until he'd starting flirting and she realized he *had* noticed her. But then she wasn't sure if his excessive flirting was genuine interest, or if he was just playing around, which sparked the roller coaster of emotions she'd been riding ever since.

"Why now?" she managed.

"Because after my father passed away and my mother had healed to the point where she was no longer struggling—

when *I* was no longer struggling—there came a moment when I looked at you and I just knew our time had come."

He lowered his face closer to hers. His hat buffered them, making it feel like they were alone, even though there were people all around them. His hand warmed her neck, sending rivers of heat down her spine, and his honest eyes held her captive. She wanted to memorize this moment. To remember the way her heart pounded so hard she knew it wanted to beat right beside his, and how he'd erased any doubts she'd had. She wanted to memorize the peace that came with the clarity of knowing Cal hadn't been toying with her at all. He'd been careful, waiting for the right time, and he'd been just as nervous as she was.

"Do you feel it, Rachel? Has our time come, or did this cowboy lose his shot with the only woman he wants?"

She didn't hesitate. Placing her hands on his broad shoulders and using them for leverage, she went up on her toes, and finally—*sweet grace, finally*—she pressed her lips to his. She was too nervous for the first touch to be anything but shaky and a little tentative. She'd wanted to kiss him for so long, she worried she'd mess it up. But then his free hand circled her waist, crushing her to him as his tongue swept across the seam of her lips, and all that nervousness fell away, unleashing years of pent-up desire. His kisses weren't frenzied or hurried. They were deep and sensual, like he wanted to savor every second as much as she did. She lifted higher on her toes, and his hand splayed across her back, keeping her flush against him. He was deliciously hard everywhere, from his powerful thighs to his muscular chest, and every tempting inch in between.

When he eased his efforts, kissing her lighter, more tenderly, she couldn't resist pushing her hands into his hair, wanting to feel more of him. It was lush and thick, and felt exactly how she'd imagined. She knocked his hat to the ground, but neither one pulled away. She didn't know how long they kissed beneath that tree, or how many hundreds of people might have seen them, and she didn't care. She was finally in Cal's arms, and she never wanted this moment to end.

Chapter Three

CAL MUST HAVE kissed Rachel at least a hundred times in the hour since they'd shared their first kiss, and the thrill was bigger, his emotions ran deeper, with each and every one since. They walked arm in arm around the festival, checking out the booths, but he was too high on Rachel to focus on anything else. They shared barbecue and fries and watched a group of kids roasting meat on sticks in the cowpoke area.

"Look how cute they are with their little cowboy hats and boots." Rachel leaned into him. "I bet you were right in the middle of all of that when you were young."

"Always," he said as they headed back toward the festivities. "There's nothing better than feeling like one of the big guys when you're a little tyke."

"I was surprised to see you with Li'l Hal this morning. Do you watch him often?"

"Are you kidding? If Hal Braden had been around, I wouldn't have been allowed to take him out today." Hal was

Rex's father, and he loved his grandkids to no end. Between him and Rex, who always seemed to have Li'l Hal in his arms, the boy rarely left his loving family circle. But today Hal and Rex were both helping to run the festival.

"I know that's true, because Jade is wondering what's going to happen when their second baby is born." A group of kids darted past, and Cal pulled her against his side. "Do you think you'll ever want a family?"

"Heck, yeah. My house already feels too quiet most days." Cal was the oldest of his siblings and was the only one to have followed his father and grandfather into the horse training business. His sister was an interior designer, and his brother was a pilot. But Cal had gotten more than just a love of horses from his father. His love for family, and the desire to have his own, had hit Cal hard recently.

He pulled Rachel closer and asked, "How about you?"

"I definitely do. When I was a kid I never thought I would want a big family. I'm so close to my parents, and being an only child, I thought there was no way a parent could love more than one child like mine love me. But, of course, you grow up and get to know families, and you realize how bountiful love is. You know how close I am with Emily and her cousins, and they have huge families. Being around them has made me want that for my kids." She pointed to the Trusty Pies and Pet Pampering booth and her eyes widened. "Have you ever had Elisabeth's River Pie?"

"Can't say that I have."

"Can we get a slice?"

He chuckled. "We can get anything your little heart desires." He leaned down for another kiss as they weaved through the crowd. "Do you feel like you missed out by not having siblings?"

"No," she answered. "I had so many friends, I didn't miss out, I don't think. But I worry about what will happen after my parents are gone, you know? I think about that sometimes, being void of family. It's a scary thought. I'll have my friends, but it would be nice to have a sibling who had been there my whole life."

She leaned against his side as they waited in line and said, "I wished I could have been there with you when you lost your father. I wanted to be."

"That was a rough time. Thank you."

"You must miss him an awful lot."

"More than you can imagine. I still see him around, you know? In the barn, and at times like these, when I'm listening for his laugh." He shrugged. "I like to think he's watching us, smiling down at us, doling out advice and shaking his head. Lord knows he's probably cursed me a million times for hitting on you so brazenly."

A sexy smile formed on her lips. "I think he'd be proud of you for finally going after what you wanted."

"Thanks, darlin'. That's a much better thought to have in

my head." He pulled her into another kiss, and her arms wound around his neck.

"About damn time."

They drew apart at his buddy Steve Johnson's voice, and Rachel blushed a red streak. Cal wanted to chase that blush right down her body and love her so thoroughly she'd blush from the memories.

"It *is* about damn time," Cal said.

"Where's Shannon?" Rachel asked.

"My fiancée ran off with a mob of girls to make candles or something."

"Candles, huh?" Rachel said with a playful glimmer in her eyes. "You should have gone with her. I hear candlemaking can be life changing."

Damn, darlin', just when I thought my night couldn't get any better, you surprise me.

"With all the wedding planning we've done, I think I've had all the life-changing events I can handle for a while." Steve waved to someone across the grass and said, "Are you in the rodeo?"

"No way." Cal could ride with the best of them, but he hadn't signed up for anything more than helping Luke, with the hopes of finally getting to spend time with Rachel. Now he was glad he'd thought ahead. "But we're going to watch it after we get a piece of Elisabeth's River Pie."

"Did you hear she's pregnant?" Steve asked.

"No!" Rachel peered around Cal and looked at Elisabeth, who was busy helping a customer decide which pie she might like. Elisabeth was married to Emily's brother, Ross. "She doesn't look pregnant, and Emily didn't say anything this morning about it."

"They just told everyone this afternoon, so Emily probably didn't know. Twelve weeks today. Shannon had some pie earlier and said, now that Elisabeth's pregnant, her pies taste even sweeter." Steve lowered his voice, as if Shannon could somehow hear him, and said, "I think it has more to do with the fact that she has an affinity for pink icing, and Elisabeth always puts some on Shannon's piece. I'll catch you guys later."

After Steve took off, they got their pie and sat at a picnic table to share it.

"Open up, darlin'." Cal held up a forkful of the creamy white chocolate with chunks of dark chocolate and whipped marshmallow cream.

She had a dreamy look in her eyes. "I feel like I'm dreaming and I'm going to wake up tomorrow and realize all of this never happened, or it was some kind of horrible joke."

Cal set the fork on the plate and straddled the bench so he was facing her. "This is as real as it gets for me, Rach. I know I waited a long time, and you're probably used to guys who move much quicker. But I needed to get my world under control before I could even hope you'd want to be in it with me."

"First, I'm not *used to* any guys," she said softly. "And second, that's really thoughtful, but everyone goes through hard times, and dealing with them together is what makes couples stronger."

"I understand that, but I wanted to be the man you deserved to have by your side, not someone who was fragmented from the very beginning of our relationship. I've got nothing standing in my way anymore. No heart-wrenching event that might take me to my knees, or family who needs me to lean on while they find their footing. At least for now. I know my mother won't live forever"—he took her hand in his—"but by then I hope we'll be so close, you'll know who I am when I'm not suffering a loss, and it'll be easier because we'll go through it together. The ball's in your court, Rachel. We'll be as real, and last as long, as you want us to."

She rose to her feet and straddled the bench in front of him. Placing her hands on his thighs, she leaned closer and gazed into his eyes. "Then I'm all in, Cal Hayden, so don't hurt me, okay?"

The grin splitting his lips was too big to stop as he took her face between his hands and said, "The only hurt you'll feel is when I get too excited and kiss you too hard, darlin'."

"That's the best kind of hurt there is."

A LITTLE WHILE later they were back at the arena with Callie, Emily and her mother, Catherine, and a handful of their other relatives, watching Wes and Cutter in the ring. The crowd was going wild as Wes and Cutter rode broncs, roped calves, and wrestled steer. Cal stood by the fence with Emily's husband, Dae, and the rest of Emily's brothers, whooping and hollering, cheering them on, while Rachel sat with the girls in the stands right behind them, gushing over her and Cal's newfound coupledom.

"Finally," Emily said as she hugged her for the tenth time in as many minutes. "We have watched you two tiptoe around what everyone else saw for so long, we were ready to lock you in a bedroom together and tell you not to come out until you had seen each other naked."

"Emily!" Rachel laughed, and Cal must have heard what Emily said, because he turned and flashed a sinful smile that set off a whirlwind of emotions inside her.

He took off his Stetson and placed it on her head, looking even more handsome with his messy blond hair setting off his eyes. The hat was warm from his head and so big it sank down low on hers. He tipped up the front of it and said, "Does my girl look hot in my hat, or what?"

"Hot and *taken*," Emily said.

"And it's about time, young man," Catherine chimed in.

"I'll have you know, this pretty gal here was on my match-making list for kissing under the mistletoe this winter."

He pressed his lips to Rachel's, then grinned at Catherine. "The only man she'll be kissin' from now on is this one, Ms. B. But if you want to set up that mistletoe around your house, I'll gladly bring my girl over and put it to good use." He chuckled and turned back toward the festivities.

"He's a feisty little devil," Catherine said. Then she reached across Emily and patted Rachel's leg. "And he's a good man, honey."

"I know," Rachel said, absently touching his hat. "I've known for a long time."

"Ow, ow, ow." Callie spread her hand over her burgeoning belly and sucked in air between clenched teeth.

"What is it?" Catherine and Emily said at once.

The color drained from Callie's face. "I've been having these pains on and off for the last few days, but they're worse tonight. We called the doctor and he said it's common to have Braxton Hicks contractions this close to my due date. But they take me by surprise every time."

Luke's wife, Daisy, leaned around Catherine and said, "He's right, Callie. Some women experience them for weeks before the birth." Daisy was a family practice physician.

"I would hate that," Callie said. "I'm due next week, and I swear if this baby is a day late, I'm going to walk from one end of Trusty to the other and back again until I go into labor."

They all laughed.

"Do you want me to get you a drink or something?" Rachel asked.

"No, thanks. The baby sits on my bladder, so if I drink, I'll have to pee, and the bathroom is halfway across the festival grounds." Callie rubbed her belly. "I can't wait to meet our baby."

"I can't wait to *spoil* your baby." Emily glanced at Dae, who was as enthralled with the rodeo as the rest of the guys, and said, "We're trying to get pregnant."

"You are?" Fiona asked. "We're talking about it, too. Jake brought it up again last night. I think being around Callie has had an effect on him."

"I think Jake's sexy wife has an effect on him," Catherine said with a wink.

"Both your babies will be so cute!" Rachel said.

Daisy smiled warmly at Catherine and said, "We're thinking about adopting."

"Really?" Emily asked. "Are you and Luke having trouble getting pregnant?"

"No. We haven't tried yet, and we still want to have babies one day," Daisy explained. "But there are so many children in other countries who need families. We feel blessed to be surrounded by so much love, and we want to share it with a baby who isn't."

"I love that," Emily said. "Dae is adopted, and we talked about going that route, but he really wants to carry on his family's heritage."

"That's understandable," Rebecca said.

"When did you decide to adopt?" Rachel asked.

"We've been talking about it for a long time, but we didn't want to tell anyone until we started the process and were sure it was even a possibility. We were going to tell you guys this afternoon, but then we didn't want to steal Elisabeth and Ross's thunder," Daisy explained.

"I'd share my thunder with you anytime." Elisabeth pushed her blond hair over her shoulder and hugged Daisy. The two blondes looked like they could be sisters.

Callie grabbed her stomach again and looked pleadingly at Daisy. "If these are practice contractions, then labor is going to stink."

"They'll give you an epidural," Daisy said. "And afterward you won't even remember the pain. You'll be too focused on the sweet little baby in your arms."

"That's what everyone tells me, but I'm not so sure." A few minutes later Callie grabbed her belly again. "Oh!" She winced. "Daisy," she pleaded. "How do you know when they're real?"

"Usually Braxton Hicks aren't painful, just uncomfortable."

"These are more than uncomfortable," Callie said.

"Are they getting worse? Coming closer together than what you've been experiencing?" Daisy asked.

"Most definitely." Callie bit her lower lip. "How much longer is the rodeo?"

"Forget the rodeo, baby girl," Catherine said. "Let's get your doctor on the phone."

Callie dug out her phone and handed it to Catherine. "Dr. Weiss should be on my recent call list."

"What can we do?" Rachel asked as panic rose in Callie's eyes.

Daisy rubbed Callie's back. "Let's get her up so she can change positions." She helped Callie to her feet. "Braxton Hicks tend to go away when you move around."

Cal turned and put a hand on Rachel's back as the girls made their way out of the crowded aisle. "Everything okay, darlin'?"

"I think so, but we're checking. Callie's having some discomfort. I'll be right back." She set his hat back on his head and gave him a quick kiss, which he deepened.

"Wow, don't ever stop that, okay?" she said before turning to join the girls.

Cal smacked her butt, and when she spun around, surprised, he blew her a kiss.

She caught up to the girls as they walked along the grass, and a few minutes later, Callie grabbed her belly again and whimpered. Suddenly there was a flurry of excitement, as

Catherine relayed what was happening to Callie's doctor, and everyone spoke at once, trying to help Callie and figure out if she was in labor.

"Okay, that's it," Daisy said, as soon as the next contraction relented. "We need to get you to the hospital. Braxton Hicks do not make it so you can't breathe. We need Wes."

"Cal can get him!" Rachel ran to Cal and grabbed the back of his shirt. He spun around and she said, "Callie's in labor! We need Wes."

"Labor?" Jake spun around. "Where is she?"

"I'll get Wes," Luke said. "Where's Daisy?"

"Daisy's with her." Rachel pointed to where she'd left the girls. "The girls are all over there, but they're a little panicky, too."

"Let me get Wes. You take care of the girls," Cal said.

Luke took one step and turned back toward Cal. "My horses?"

"I've got this, Luke. Give me your truck keys. I'll get the horses situated, then bring your truck back here. Can you get a ride back?" Cal asked.

"I can get a ride." Luke handed him his keys. "Daisy has a set of keys, so just lock these in the glove compartment. Thanks, man."

"No problem. Go be with your family."

"I'll help you," Rachel offered as Luke and his brothers bolted toward the girls.

Cal took her hand and said, "Let's go, beautiful."

He plowed through the crowd, hanging on tight to her hand all the way up to the gates to the arena. He looked larger than life, confident, and in charge as he relayed the information to a burly guy in a flannel shirt, who then spoke into a radio, and moments later, another guy was standing on a platform waving a white flag and pointing at Wes.

Wes dismounted his horse, handed the reins to another guy, and ran out of the ring, wide-eyed and hopped up on adrenaline. He panted out, "What's up?"

Cal was dead calm and focused as he said, "Callie's in labor. You've got to go."

"Holy shit. We're in labor!" Wes slapped Cal on the back, hugged Rachel, and hollered, "We're in labor!" He took off like his feet were on fire in Callie's direction.

Rachel grabbed her chest to try to slow her racing heart. "How can you be so calm?"

Cal gathered her in his arms and gazed into her eyes, sending her already frantic heart into overdrive. "Darlin' when you grow up on a ranch, you learn quickly that in times of crisis, panicking spooks people as much as it does animals."

"Well, that's impressive. I don't know if I'll ever be able to be that calm when everyone else is going crazy."

"Lucky for you, you won't need to. I'll be right there by your side, holding you tight and keeping you steady in the midst of the stampede."

As he lowered his lips to hers, she silently prayed for a stampede.

Chapter Four

AFTER THE RODEO, Cal helped Cutter load Wes's horses
into the trailer so he could take them to the dude ranch, and
Rachel helped carry tack and blankets. She wasn't afraid to
get her hands dirty, which he loved. She helped him load
Luke's horses into his trailer, and once they were safely
situated, Cal took her hand and led her out of the barn,
toward the craft tent.

"The festival is closing soon," she said, hurrying to keep
up with his long strides. "Don't we have to take care of
Luke's horses?"

"We do, and we will." He stole a quick kiss and said,
"But first we need to get our candles."

"Oh gosh, I totally forgot with all the excitement."

They rushed across the fairgrounds and got to the crafts
tent just as the candlemaking booth was closing down. They
retrieved the candles and put them in Cal's truck.

On the way back to the trailer, Cal stopped and gathered

Rachel in his arms. "I'm sorry our night's been hijacked."

She returned his embrace and said, "I'm not. I got to see you doing all the things you love, and the way you jumped in without hesitation to help Luke and Wes? Seeing that was almost as much of a heartwarmer as seeing you with Li'l Hal."

He brushed his lips over hers, feeling his emotions swell. "Heartwarmer, huh? What do I have to do to turn that heartwarming into an aphrodisiac?"

"You already cornered that market by simply being yourself. No props necessary."

"Darlin', that's about the sweetest thing I've ever heard." He touched his lips to hers again, and she pushed her hands into his hair as she'd done earlier, knocking his hat to the ground. They both smiled into the kiss.

"Want to try my shirt next?"

"Maybe," she whispered. "But I think we need to kiss some more."

She didn't have to ask twice.

An hour later they arrived at Luke's ranch. Rachel helped Cal get the horses situated in the barn.

"Hey, darlin'," he said as she petted one of the horses. "I know Luke likes to calm his girls down for the night after events, kind of like tucking your kids into bed. Would you mind if I took a few minutes to brush the two that were in the show? It's a really mellow time for the horses. One of my favorite times of the day, although I don't usually do it this late."

"I don't mind." She came to him, hooking her finger through his belt loop. "Think you can teach me how? I've never taken care of a horse."

"Really? Sweetheart, I'd love to show you how." He gathered her in his arms again and said, "You are even more remarkable than I thought you were."

"Because I want to learn to do the things that you take pleasure in?"

"You'd best be careful choosing your words, because what you just said? Mm-mm. That can be taken the wrong way."

"How do you know it's not meant to be taken that way?" She went up on her toes and kissed him.

His entire body heated up.

"Down, boy," she whispered as their lips parted.

"You're torturing me, baby. Pure, exquisite torture."

She giggled as he grabbed a brush and they went into one of the stalls.

"This is Chelsea." He stroked the horse's cheek, and the horse pressed her muzzle to his chest. "Hey there, sweet girl. You did a great job today. We're going to brush you down, nice and easy." He moved the horse's mane to the far side of her neck and said, "Chelsea's a tobiano. See how her base coat is black and the white patches cross over her spine?"

When Cal groomed a horse, he was completely focused

on the animal, but as he moved behind Rachel and set the brush in her hand, his body grazed hers. Her sweet scent overrode the familiar smell of the barn, and he had trouble concentrating on anything *but* her.

"Gypsy horses have thicker coats than other horses," he explained, needing to take his mind off how soft Rachel's body was. He placed his hand over hers and brought the brush to the horse's neck. "They appreciate a good brushing because they tend to get itchy. Usually I'd start with a curry comb to bring the dirt to the surface, but we're calming her down, not grooming her. You want to use long, *slow* strokes for relaxation." Holding Rachel's hand over the brush, he moved it down Chelsea's neck. "Like this."

"Long and slow," she repeated breathlessly.

"That's it," he said as she brushed the horse.

Her every move brought their bodies closer together, heating him up anew. She smelled so sweet, and he wanted her so bad, he couldn't resist releasing her hand and gathering her hair over one shoulder. As he lowered his mouth to her neck, pressing a kiss there, her hand stilled. He did it again, and her breath left her lungs on a long, nearly silent sigh. She leaned back, and he knew she could feel how hard he was. And damn did she feel good. He felt a little guilty, kissing her when she'd asked to learn how to care for the horse. He reluctantly put space between them.

He placed his hand over hers and continued brushing the

horse with her. But she leaned into him again, and he felt her heart beating hard and fast through her back.

"Like this?" she asked softly.

"Perfect."

She leaned her head to the side, exposing the creamy expanse of her neck, and he couldn't resist kissing her again. "You smell like flowers." He inhaled deeply and pressed his lips beside her ear. "So sweet."

Her hand slowed again, and she said, "Premiere, by Gucci. It's my favorite."

"And mine now."

He kissed her cheek again, and his body thrummed with desire. He kissed her neck, closing his eyes and watching scenes play out of stripping her down and making love to her right there in the barn. His eyes flew open as reality crashed in. This wasn't *his* barn. The last thing he wanted to do was break their connection, but he forced himself to move beside her. She was so beautiful as she concentrated on the horse, stealing glances at him, and blushing with each one. Cal's hands itched to touch her. He grabbed a second brush and moved to the other side of the horse, needing a barrier between them before he crossed a line he shouldn't.

"Can you do that?" she asked. "Brush both sides at once without bothering the horse?"

"Sure. We're supposed to be connecting with her. It's safer if I'm over here."

Her pale green eyes filled with desire, and it took all of his concentration not to forget the brushing altogether.

They worked in silence for a few minutes, the heat between them as palpable as the horse. Rachel must have felt it, too, because with a shaky voice, she asked, "Do you groom your horses at night?"

"Not usually. But I like to hang out with the horses in the evening. It's peaceful, and horses are social animals. They like having me around."

"I like having you around, too." Her sexy eyes darted to him.

They stole furtive glances over the horse's back as they finished brushing her.

"What about her legs?" Rachel asked when he came to her side.

"We're just tucking her in, so there's no need."

They left Chelsea's stall and went to care for the other horse who had been in the show. "This is Shaley, a real sweetie. Like you." He pulled Rachel closer and kissed her, long and deep. It was the type of kiss that left no room for doubt of how much more he wanted. And when their lips parted, he didn't want to let her go. But Cal was a man of his word, and Luke was counting on him. And though Luke didn't ask him to brush the horses, he couldn't take care of one and not the other.

He forced himself to take a step back, and they went to

work brushing Shaley. They talked about Callie and Wes, and the festival, which made the time pass quicker. Cal finished before Rachel did, and he wrapped his arms around her from behind as she brushed the horse.

He knew he shouldn't, but he kissed her cheek and whispered in her ear, "Your skin is so soft. I've wanted to touch it, to kiss you, for so long."

Her hand slowed, and he said, "I'm sorry for distracting you. It's not fair to the horse or to us. I just can't resist you."

"If I promise not to stop brushing, will you keep kissing me?" she asked softly.

"I don't think I'll ever be able to deny you a thing, darlin'." He lowered his lips to her neck again, and he opened his mouth, giving her neck a little suck. Her eyelids fluttered closed, and he drew back. "Too much?"

"No," she said breathlessly. "*Please...*"

"Remind me never to offer to brush someone else's horse again, okay, darlin'?"

As he lowered his mouth to her neck, kissing and licking, she breathed harder, swallowed several times, but she never stopped brushing the horse, and that tugged at his heart. He put his hand on her hip, holding her against him as he moved the collar of her sweater to the side, baring her beautiful shoulder, and kissed her there. Desire welled up inside him, throbbing through his veins like fire. He opened his mouth wider, grazing her neck with his teeth, and pressed his hand to her waist, then higher. His thumbs brushed the sides of her breasts, and she inhaled a ragged breath. His hands moved over her stomach, down the front of her thighs, as he continued his exploration of her soft, warm shoulder, tasting his way up the column of her neck, until they were both barely breathing and Rachel was trembling all over.

"I'm sorry," he said half-heartedly. "You're supposed to feel a connection with the horse." He lowered his hands to her waist and stepped back.

"I feel a connection," she whispered. "With you both."

The horse looked back at them, as if to say, *I'm good. You two can go now.*

"This isn't fair to her—or to us." He took Rachel's hand and left the stall. They kissed as he hurriedly put away the brushes and secured the barn, and then they ran back to the truck, holding hands and laughing. When they reached it, he couldn't wait another second. He took her in his arms and crashed his mouth over hers. She grabbed his shoulders, and her legs circled his waist as they ate at each other's mouths. She tasted hot and sweet, and she felt like heaven in his arms. And those noises she made totally *wrecked* him, but they were standing outside Luke's house, and there was no endgame, not here.

He tore his mouth away and said, "We're at Luke's."

"I know. We should have thought to bring two cars. We have to take his truck back." A spark of heat shone in her eyes and she said, "Drive fast."

RACHEL WAS SO nervous on the drive back to the fairgrounds, she could barely breathe. She had a feeling that was going to happen a lot around Cal. He kept her close, driving with one arm around her, his big hand palming her shoulder. The air around them vibrated with sexual tension. At the stoplights, there were no words, only hungry kisses and mournful noises when the light changed and they were forced to part. By the time they reached the fairgrounds she was a tingling bundle of desire. The fairgrounds were dark, and the parking lot was empty, save for a few cars, which Rachel recognized as belonging to Emily and her relatives. She'd sent a quick text to Emily earlier asking about Callie, and Emily had said she was still in labor and that it might be a while. She promised to text as soon as the baby was born. Rachel couldn't help but think how serendipitous it was that she and Cal's relationship was coming to life the same day Callie was giving birth.

They parked Luke's truck near the other cars, and as they hurried toward Cal's truck, he hauled her against him.

"Is your car here?"

"No. Emily drove me over."

He gazed into her eyes, and the silence stretched between them until it pulsed like a heartbeat.

He touched his forehead to hers and said, "I don't want to pressure you, but I don't want this night to end."

She didn't know if she could muster the courage to say what she felt, but she was afraid not to. When she opened her mouth to speak, the truth came easily, and she knew it was not only the right thing to say, but it was the *only* thing. "Then take me home with you, because I don't want it to end, either."

Twenty heart-pounding minutes later, they were carrying their candles up Cal's driveaway. She glanced at Cal. His strong features looked even more handsome against the moonlight spilling over the crest of the mountains in the distance. He tipped his face toward hers, and her stomach went a little crazy. Maybe it was the way her emotions swelled every time he looked at her, or the way his kisses turned her inside out. Or maybe it was how he made everything sound romantic and lovely. She didn't know if it was Cal, or the night, or both, but she had lived in Trusty all her life and she'd never seen such an incredible view as the one before her.

"Having second thoughts?" he asked carefully.

"Not on your life," she said honestly, earning a toe-curling smile.

He draped his arm over her shoulder, and the vanilla scent of the candle coalesced with the unique scent of Cal. She didn't wait for him to draw her closer. She turned to him, ready for his kiss. His mouth was soft as silk, his kisses insistent, but it was the sounds of desire rumbling up his throat that sent a rush of heat through her core.

"Come with me, darlin'," he said against her lips, and continued kissing her as they made their way up the front steps and into the screened porch.

He broke their connection only long enough to tuck one of the candles between his arm and his side and unlock the front door. Her gaze landed on the metal sign hanging above two rocking chairs on the porch, which read LONG AFTER THE WIND LEAVES MY SAILS, MY LOVE FOR MY FAMILY WILL STILL PREVAIL. Her heart skipped a beat.

"You have the sign I had made for your father."

He followed her gaze to the sign above the chairs. "*You* had that made?"

She nodded. "I saw him at the park with your mother right before he got sick. We sat on a bench chatting for a long time that afternoon. Your dad told me stories about when you and your brother and sister were younger. It was like he was reliving those memories, and I could see how much he enjoyed sharing them. He said that to me, that quote on the sign. I loved it so much, and I thought it said a lot about him, and your family. That's why I had it made when he got sick. I was going to paint it, like I do with all the others, but paint chips, and I thought, if he couldn't live forever, at least his thoughts could. My friend's father works with metal, and he made it for me."

Cal put his arms around her again, and longing rose in his eyes. "He gave it to me shortly before he died. That sign pulled me through some really tough times. Thank you."

He held her close as they went inside, and her senses filled with the woodsy scent of his home. It felt rustic, with dark hardwood floors, a wide stone fireplace, and rough beams lining the high ceilings. Two wall sconces sprayed light onto the stones around the fireplace, and a plush brown couch and leather chair sat atop a thick beige throw rug. On the far side of the room, a door was open, through which she saw the foot of a bed. Her nerves tingled, and she shifted her gaze to a stairway in the corner of the room, which led to a loft with a desk and a chair. Just beyond, an open barn-wood door led to another room. As she walked into the room, she noticed bookshelves littered with family photos off to her left and a tastefully decorated kitchen. She'd never wondered what Cal's house might be like, but now that she was there, she saw it suited him perfectly. Neat, masculine, and cozy. The deep couch beckoned to be curled up on with a good book.

"I like your place," she said as he set the candles he was holding on the mantel.

"Thanks." He smiled and took her candles from her, placing them on the hearth. He lit the candles and turned off the lights beside the fireplace. "I like it more now that you're here."

He pulled his cell phone from his pocket, focusing on that for a minute, before placing it next to the candles on the mantel and gathering her in his arms. "We missed the band at the festival."

The song "In Case You Didn't Know," by Brett Young streamed from his phone, and she melted against him. It was one of her favorite songs, and she knew that every time she heard it from now on, she'd remember this moment. Cal was a magnificent dancer. She'd longed to be in his arms every time she'd seen him dancing with their friends. She finally understood why he'd never asked her to dance. She'd never know what might have happened if they'd gotten together sooner, but she took comfort in knowing that Cal knew himself well enough to wait until the time was right. And when she gazed into his eyes, the emotions swimming in them made her fall even harder for him.

"Every word of this song is for you Rachel." He sang the lyrics word for word, telling her how crazy he was about her and how he couldn't live without her.

His voice was laced with honesty, and when he said she'd had his heart a long time ago, she said, "You had mine, too, Cal."

His mouth came down over hers as they swayed to the music, their bodies pressed tightly together. Her hands moved down his back, to the butt she'd been gawking at for so long, it was etched in her mind. He smiled against her mouth, and she slid her hands into his back pockets, keeping him close. His arousal pressed against her belly as their tongues tangled, and his hands moved up her body and into her hair. Oh, how she loved his big, strong hands on her. His fingers threaded into her hair as he took the kiss deeper. She felt their connection snaking through her, and she lost herself in his taste, the feel of his body, and the love winding around them like a bow.

She was vaguely aware of the song ending and the next beginning as their kisses turned hungrier, their hands more possessive. She rocked against him, and when one of his hands clutched her bottom, she heard herself moan. She didn't think as she pushed her hands beneath the sides of his shirt, feeling his muscles flex and bunch against her palms. His hips pulsed, his cock temptingly hard, and those sinful noises he made amped up her arousal. When his hand moved down her butt and his long fingers played at the seam between her legs, she felt herself go damp.

She'd waited so long for this, wanting to kiss him, to touch him, to be *his*, she threw caution to the wind, not even caring that she was making herself into a liar, and said, "Love me, Cal. Make me yours."

Chapter Five

CAL WAS FAIRLY certain he'd died and gone to heaven, but when he looked into Rachel's eyes, he felt more alive than ever before. He took her beautiful face between his hands, and the emotions looking back at him confirmed he wasn't alone in the deep-seated feelings consuming him. He kissed her softly and said, "Before I touch you the way I want to, before our bodies come together for the very first time, you need to know that I love you, Rachel Gray. I've loved you for so long. I see our future together, our babies, their proms and weddings. I see *us*, Rachel, old and wrinkled, sitting on the porch watching our grandchildren. And in my heart, I know I will love you more with every passing day."

"Oh, Cal. I've loved you just as long, if not longer."

Her breathy voice sang through him, her words filling the pieces of himself he'd left open for only her to claim.

He looked at the candles, wondering how he could get them into the bedroom without breaking their momentum.

There was no way he was going to make love to her for the first time on the floor or couch.

He kissed her again. "You deserve rose petals on the bed, the finest stereo playing in the background, and shooting stars, but all I have are candles and my phone. I want to love you in my bed, Rachel, but I'm not cool enough to figure out how to carry all the candles and the phone without asking for help. I'm sorry, darlin', but if you carry two candles, I'll get the rest."

She laughed softly and pressed a kiss to the center of his chest. "You probably don't realize this, but everything you just said is more romantic than rose petals and shooting stars." A heart-melting smile formed on her lips as she reached for two of the candles.

They carried them into the bedroom, and set them, and his phone, on the nightstand. Rachel fidgeted nervously with the edge of her sweater, watching him move toward her. He'd dreamed of her in his bed for so long, he was nervous, too. He ran his fingers through her long hair, swaying to the music as he wrapped her in his arms, and they fell into a sensual dance to "Heartache on the Dance Floor." Her hips and shoulders moved to the beat as their mouths came together again like they'd never been apart. Soon they were so lost in the moment, the only beat he heard was the blood rushing through his head. He kissed her mouth, her jaw, her cheeks, whispering between each one, "Waited so long"…"Love you"…"Want you with me." Every word was met with a seductive sound of her own, a rock of her hips, a "Yes, please."

He eased her sweater over her head, losing his breath at the sight of his girl in a pink lace bra. She blushed from her chest to her cheeks even as she pushed eagerly at his shirt. He pulled it off and tossed it aside. Her gaze moved over his chest and abs, and lower, fueling his need for her.

"God you're beautiful," he said as he pulled her close again and kissed her deeply.

Her hands moved up his sides, over his back. Every touch stoked the raging inferno inside him. He lifted her into his arms, earning another sweet laugh. As he laid her on the bed, she smiled up at him, happiness radiating off her so strongly, it seeped beneath his skin and warmed him to his core.

"Shoes," she whispered with a near silent giggle as she pointed at their feet.

He chuckled as he moved to the edge of the bed and took off his boots and socks. Then he removed hers and crawled over her. "I don't know where to start. I want to cherish every inch of you, to memorize every luscious curve and dip of your body. But I also want to tear off your clothes and make love to you, because going slow is going to be really, really hard." That earned him another lusty smile.

"I like really, really hard," she said quietly.

"Sweetness between the sheets," he said without thinking,

and pressed his lips to hers in another passionate kiss.

He drew back with her lower lip between his teeth, giving it a gentle tug. "Sweet with a little heat coming right up."

He dusted kisses down her neck and over her breastbone, dragged his tongue along the skin just above the lace trim on her bra, bringing rise to goose bumps. She arched beneath him, her fingers digging into his back.

"Ah, my girl likes that." He did it again on the other side, and she made a whimpering sound that sparked between his legs.

He unhooked the front clasp of her bra and used his teeth to move the cups to the sides, exposing her gorgeous breasts. His eyes flicked up to hers, to make sure she was still on the same page, but her eyes were closed, her cheeks flushed. When she bowed off the bed and pushed down on his shoulders, he knew they were in sync. He lowered his mouth to one breast, filling his hand with the other, and teased over her nipple with his tongue. The tight bud was too alluring just to tease; he sealed his mouth over it and sucked.

"Oh!" she cried out, and he stilled. "Don't stop. Feels so good." She pushed on his shoulders again.

He didn't hold back as he sucked her breast into his mouth again and took her other nipple between his finger and thumb, gently pulling and squeezing, earning more sinful sounds, which made his cock throb. He lavished each breast with openmouthed kisses until she was rocking her hips, mewling, and writhing beneath him. Her sexy sounds made him lose his mind. He kissed and licked his way down her belly, sucking and tasting her flesh as he went. His hands played over her breasts, her ribs, and finally came to rest on her hips as he sucked the soft skin beside her belly button into his mouth, leaving a mark there. *His* mark.

Her fingers dug into the covers as he moved lower, kissing her on top of her jeans, around her thighs, eyeing her as his lips met the damp denim between her legs. He wanted to tear her jeans off but felt the need to check in again. He didn't want to screw this up. He moved swiftly up her body, pressing his shaft against her center, and kissed her urgently. He buried his fingers in her hair, intensifying the kiss. When they finally came up for air, they were both breathless.

"If you want me to stop, tell me now, darlin'. Because once I get my mouth on you, there's no stopping."

She looked up at him with determination and desire welling in her eyes. "I don't want you to stop. Not now, not ever."

"Aw, baby."

He claimed her mouth again, pouring his heart into their kisses, before loving his way down her gorgeous body. He showered her with kisses and made quick work of ridding her of her jeans and—*holy Christ*—a pink thong. She spread her legs, accommodating his broad body. Her eyes were closed, her lips pink from their heated kisses, and her fingers curled into the covers. He reached for her hand and turned it over, placing his fingers over hers. She curled hers up and he curled his down, locking their hands, as they sealed their love.

He kissed her inner thighs, the scent of her arousal reeling him in. He dragged his tongue along the crease between her thighs and her glistening sex, earning another pleading sound. She clung to his hand as he lowered his mouth to her sex, taking his first taste of her sweetness. A long, surrendering moan slipped from her lips, spurring him on. He loved her with his mouth, devouring her sex with plundering thrusts of his tongue into her tight heat, each one earning another haughty noise. He brought his free hand into play, teasing over the nerves that made her thighs flex and her hips buck off the mattress. He stayed right with her, loving and taunting, feeling her body tremble beneath him. Her breathing came in stilted gusts as he slipped his fingers inside her, seeking the magical spot that would take her higher. He took her clit between his teeth at the same moment he crooked his fingers, completely lost in her. She rocked and moaned and pleaded, and when he sealed his mouth over her sex, his fingers still inside her, she shattered against it.

"Cal!" she cried out. "*Oh God! Oh—*"

Her sex clenched tight and perfect around his fingers as he devoured her sweet arousal, taking his fill and earning more quivers and quakes.

"Don't stop, Cal. Please don't stop."

He wasn't about to stop, especially not when the arc of her voice and the pulsing of her hips told him she was on the verge of another orgasm. He unlinked their hands so he could hold her hips to the mattress as he feasted on her, sending her soaring once again. Indiscernible sounds filled the room as she came, and he soaked in every last one.

"I need *you*," she pleaded, reaching for him with trembling hands.

He'd never stripped so fast as he did right then. He came down over her, his cock resting against her slick heat. Their mouths came together in a feverish storm of desperation and greed.

"Love you so much," he said between kisses.

"Me too."

"I need you, baby." He pulled open his nightstand to grab a condom.

She touched his arm and said, "I'm on the pill."

He closed his eyes for a beat, thanking the heavens above, because the thought of anything separating them pained him. He kissed her slowly and sensually, but within seconds they were kissing with savage intensity once again. Their kisses went on and on, and it was heaven and hell holding back from entering her, but he needed—wanted—her to hear the truth before they crossed that bridge.

He forced himself to slow down enough to tell her what he needed her to know. "I haven't been with anyone since before my father died. There's been only you in my heart and, I hoped one day, in my life, baby."

He lowered his mouth to hers as their bodies came together. She was so tight, so warm and soft inside, he felt like she was made for him. It took effort to bury himself completely, and when he gazed into her eyes, he wondered if this was her first time.

"Baby…?"

"I've only been with one other guy," she said softly. "It was a *really* long time ago."

"Am I hurting you?"

Her lips curved up in a smile, and she said, "No. You're completing me."

His heart swelled, and he pushed his arms beneath her, cradling her against him, wanting them to be as close as they possibly could. He pressed his lips to hers, and from that moment on there were no thoughts, no words, only love. Their bodies moved in exquisite harmony, slow and careful, then fast and eager, as they explored each other's bodies. He learned the soft lines of her hips and waist, the warmth of the crook of her knee as he lifted it to his hip, loving her deeper. Her fingers played over his ass and back, along his neck, as they made out like they might never get another chance. When he pushed his hands beneath her hips, lifting her so he could hit the spot that sent her soaring, his name flew from her lips like a prayer, and he followed her into oblivion, surrendering to his own powerful release.

Long after they came down from the clouds, they lay tangled together, with Rachel's head tucked against Cal's shoulder as she slept. He listened to the soft cadence of her breathing. Shadows danced over the bed from the candles they'd made together and music streamed from his phone. Cal felt at peace for the first time since he'd lost his father. He closed his eyes, visions of Rachel carrying him into the numbed sleep of a man who had everything he'd ever wanted right there by his side.

Chapter Six

RACHEL STARTLED AWAKE to the sound of text messages rolling in one after another. She blinked the haze of sleep from her eyes and saddened at the thought of prying herself from Cal's arms. They'd woken up a few hours ago and made love a second time, and now that she was awake again, her girly parts were throwing a party, ready for an encore performance. She snuggled in closer when the dinging stopped, but a few seconds later, more texts sounded. She tried to ease out of his arms without waking him, but he tightened his hold on her, and she couldn't suppress her smile.

"Let it go," he said in a drowsy voice.

"What if it's important?"

He rolled her onto her back and smiled down at her with a loving look in his eyes. "More important than this?"

He rocked his hard length against her and dipped his

head beneath the blanket. His mouth came down over her breast, and he gave it a long *suck*, alighting flames beneath her skin.

"Oh God. I hope not," she said.

She bent her knees, lifting her hips to greet him. Happiness flowed through her as he filled her inch by blessed inch and they found their tempo. His hands skimmed down her sides and beneath her bottom. Oh, how she loved the feel of him inside her, holding her, *surrounding* her. He loved her so thoroughly, pure, explosive pleasure radiated down her limbs, to the very tips of her fingers and toes. They kissed and loved and tasted until they were both *almost* too spent to move—and then he rolled over on his back and a rush of adrenaline accompanied the new, titillating position. She rode him slowly at first, but the pressure, the feel of his hands on her breasts, was too much, and her carnal desires took over. Her hips bucked, hard and fast, sending them both spiraling into ecstasy. Her orgasm went on and on, and somewhere in the back of her mind she cataloged the fantastic position as she collapsed against him, drowning in a flood of their love.

After her breathing calmed and they came back to earth, she wiggled out of his arms to use the bathroom. She sat at the edge of the bed and grabbed her jeans from the floor to retrieve her phone. There were several new messages from Emily and Shannon.

Cal wrapped his arms around her from behind as she opened one of them, and a picture of Callie and Wes and their new baby filled her screen. The caption beneath it read, *Meet Belle Catherine Braden!*

"Oh my gosh. Look!" She showed Cal the picture. "She's so precious. Look at those cheeks. I just want to kiss them. And her wispy hair." The picture sent her right back up to the clouds, feeling dreamy and happy as she scrolled through more pictures and texts. "Belle Catherine, eight pounds, two ounces. Callie loves fairy tales. She told me that when she and Wes first started dating, he threw her a ball and sent her a dress like Belle's from *Beauty and the Beast*. I love that they named their daughter Belle Catherine after Callie's favorite things and Wes's mom. That's so sweet."

"That is sweet, and that baby girl sure is beautiful. Callie and Wes look exhausted but elated. I can't wait for that."

"I thought I would have exhausted you by now," she teased as she scrolled through more pictures, showing each of them to Cal.

He kissed her shoulder. "You thrill me, darlin'. You don't exhaust me. I'm looking forward to having a family. That's what it's all about, right? We spend years going to school, making a name for ourselves, figuring out who we are. But what good is all of that if you don't share it with someone you love and pass on your life lessons to the next generation of crazy kids that'll ignore you and sneak out at night causing trouble?"

She laughed. "I never snuck out at night."

"You would have if I'd have known you back then. I would have gotten you in all sorts of trouble."

"Somehow I don't believe that."

"Aw, come on. Let me pretend to be a badass."

"You've got the baddest ass around, but you're not a troublemaker." She kissed him and headed for the bathroom.

"Spend the day with me," he called after her. "Let's watch the sunrise and see what kind of trouble we can stir up together."

She used the bathroom, then came out with a towel wrapped around her. "I'd love to." She crooked her finger, beckoning him. "After our shower."

He stood, and six-plus feet of naked cowboy strode toward her. His cock was still half hard, nestled on a tuft of blond hair between his powerful thighs. Her mouth went dry as he closed the distance between them. His hair was tousled, hanging over his eyes, which were drilling a hole right through her. He bent to kiss her, and as she put her arms around his neck, her towel dropped to the ground. She wasn't even a little embarrassed.

She ran her fingers through his hair. She loved knowing she could do that as much as she wanted from now on. "Is it weird that I feel like I've been here forever?"

"No, because you've *belonged* here forever."

A LITTLE WHILE later, after knocking shower sex off their bucket list, Rachel and Cal sat on his back porch wrapped in a blanket, watching the sun rise over the mountains. She could hardly believe it had been less than twenty-four hours since they'd come together. She leaned against Cal, thinking of all they'd shared, and just as the sun spilled over the fields, her stomach growled.

"All that lovin's got you hungry," he teased, and kissed her neck.

"Starving, actually."

He rose to his feet and brought her up with him. "Then, come on, darlin'. Let's hit the diner. Then we can come back here and I'll introduce you to my horses."

"The last time I went with you into a barn, I learned the art of seduction." She put her arm around his waist as they went inside to retrieve his keys.

He groped her butt and said, "You're a remarkable student. Maybe if you're good I'll show you my hayloft."

"And if I'm *bad*?" She waggled her brows, and he hauled her against him, making her laugh.

"Careful, baby, or we may never make it to the diner, much less the barn."

THEY MADE IT into town, though they were delayed by hungry kisses in the driveway, at the stoplights, and in the parking lot. Rachel couldn't get enough of Cal, and apparently he couldn't get enough of her, either, because as they headed into the diner, he leaned in for another kiss.

"Well, well," Margie said as she filled a mug with coffee. "What do we have here? I seem to remember that brown sweater from yesterday, Miss Gray."

Rachel felt her eyes widen. "I…um…"

Cal tightened his hold on her and said, "She was helping me with—"

"With my horses," Luke said loudly as he rose from a booth in the corner, where he was sitting with Daisy, Emily, Dae, Jake, and Fiona, all of whom were watching them with appreciative smiles. "They were taking care of my girls."

"Is that what they're calling it now?" Margie shook her head. "Squeeze on in for breakfast with the Bradens, honey. You too, cowboy," she said to Cal. "I'll be right over to take your orders."

Jake and Luke moved a table beside the booth so they

could all sit together.

Ross and Elisabeth blew through the diner doors with Catherine on their heels.

"Hey, you guys. Sorry we're late." Elisabeth winked at Rachel and said, "Nice sweater."

A knowing smile spread across Catherine's lips. "Well, it's an even better morning than I'd thought. Did you see the pictures of the baby?"

"Yes! Oh my gosh, she's so beautiful!" Rachel said, glad for the change of subject. "How is Callie feeling?"

"Tired," Catherine said as she sat down. "But happy."

Fiona scooted over so Jake could sit beside her. "She said Daisy was right. She forgot the pain of childbirth the minute they put Belle in her hands."

"*Chubbers*," Jake said with a smirk.

"Jake." Catherine shook her head.

"What?" Jake splayed his hands. "She's adorably chubby. I think chubbers is cute, don't you?"

"I think Wes is going to beat your ass if he hears you say that," Luke said as he sat down next to Daisy.

"Maybe after he comes down from the baby high he's on." Dae flicked his chin, sending his dark hair out of his eyes. "Wes has got more energy than you can imagine. I'm afraid he'll crash hard at some point."

"We'll all crash hard after last night," Fiona said. "Poor

Callie was in labor for hours."

Cal leaned closer to Rachel and whispered, "I'd like to crash into you."

Rachel felt her cheeks flush.

Margie came over to the table, eyeing Cal and Rachel. "So, I hear we have a new Braden baby and a new Hayden couple. Trusty just got a little bit happier."

Rachel smiled up at her and leaned against Cal's shoulder. "Are you going to embarrass me every time I come in here now?"

"That depends," Margie said with a mischievous glint in her eyes. "Did you guys get together last night or this morning?"

Cal sat up a little straighter. "That's private information, Margie."

"Private and important." Margie pulled a handful of folded papers from the pocket of her pink waitress uniform. "We've got big bucks riding on this information."

"What?" Rachel snapped.

The girls lifted their menus and hid behind them.

"Big bucks? What is going on? Emily? Daisy?" Rachel saw Ross slip a few dollars to Luke. "Ross? You too?"

"Sorry, Rachel, but see the way Cal's looking at you? He's been doing that for months." Ross nodded toward Cal. "You've turned him inside out. The last time I looked at a woman that way, I married her."

"I love you, Rossie," Elisabeth said, and leaned in to kiss him.

"But you guys *bet* on us. That feels so wrong." And kind of funny, but Rachel didn't want to admit that.

"Now, don't get yourself all up in a tither," Margie said. "We might have made a friendly wager after you and Cowboy were in here last month making eyes at each other."

"Last *month*?" Rachel said.

Cal chuckled.

"Cal! Really?" She glared at him. "You're laughing about this?"

He schooled his expression, but his lips tipped up again. "I can't help it. We both knew we belonged together. They must have seen it, too. That doesn't surprise me. Darlin', a love like ours comes only once in a lifetime, and it's too big to go unnoticed."

"Aw," Daisy said. "That's so romantic."

"It is romantic," Rachel admitted. Everything he said touched her. "But doesn't it bother you that they bet on us?"

"Why? They know us. They love us." Cal pulled her closer as their friends mumbled their agreement. He gazed into her eyes like he'd done a hundred times over the past twenty-four hours and said, "I'd bet on us every single time for the rest of our lives."

As he lowered his lips to hers, their friends cheered, and Margie said, "Well, that match is done. Who's next?"

Continue reading for more Bradens!

But first, meet Belle Catherine Braden!

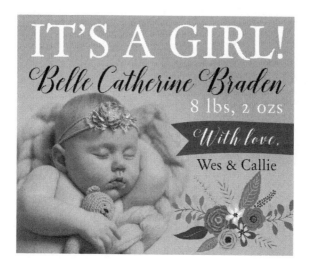

Want More Bradens?

If you'd like to learn more about the Bradens at Trusty, Colorado, you can start with the first book in that series, Luke and Daisy's love story, TAKEN BY LOVE (FREE in digital format at the time of this printing. Preview included below), or start with the very first book in the Love in Bloom big-family romance collection, SISTERS IN LOVE (FREE in digital format at the time of this printing), and get to know all of our hunky heroes and sassy heroines. Characters within the Love in Bloom family cross over and appear in other family series, so you never miss an engagement, wedding, or birth. All Love in Bloom novels may be enjoyed as stand-alone romances. Jump in anytime!

Fall in love with Luke and Daisy in
TAKEN BY LOVE

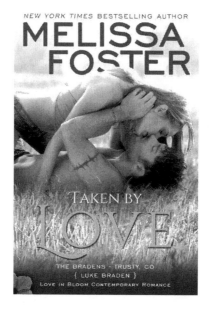

Chapter One

DAISY HONEY JUGGLED a cup of coffee, a cake she'd bought for her mother, a bag of two chocolate-dipped doughnuts—because a girl's gotta have something sweet in her life, and this was about all the sweetness she had time for at the moment—and her keys.

"You sure you got that, sugar?" Margie Holmes had worked at the Town Diner for as long as Daisy could remember. With her outdated feathered hairstyle and old-fashioned, pink waitress uniform, Margie was as much a landmark in Trusty, Colorado, as the backdrop of the Colorado Mountains and the miles and miles of farms and ranches. Trusty was a far cry from Philly, where Daisy had just completed her medical residency in family practice, and it was the last place she wanted to be.

Daisy glanced at the clock. She had ten minutes to get to work. Work. If she could call working as a temporary doctor at the Trusty Urgent Care Clinic work. She'd worked damn hard to obtain her medical degree with the hopes of leaving the Podunk town behind, but the idea of relocating had been delayed when her father fell off the tractor and injured his back. She'd never turn her back on her family, even if she'd rather be starting her career elsewhere. She supposed it was good timing—if there was such a thing. Daisy had been offered permanent positions in Chicago and New York, and she had four weeks to accept or decline the offers. She hoped by then her father would either have hired someone to manage the farm or decided if he was going to sell—an idea she was having a difficult time stomaching, since the farm had been in her family for generations. Since the closest hospital or family physician was forty-five minutes away and the urgent care clinic picked up the slack in the small town, Daisy was happy to have found temporary employment in her field even if it wasn't ideal.

"Yeah, I've got it. Thanks for the cake, Margie. Mom will love it." She pushed the door open with her butt—thank you, doughnuts—just as someone tugged it open, causing her to stumble. As if in slow motion, the cake tipped to the side. Daisy slammed her eyes shut to avoid seeing the beautiful triple-layer chocolate-almond cake crash to the ground.

There was no telltale clunk! of the box hitting the floor. She opened one eye and was met with a pair of muscled pecs attached to broad shoulders and six foot something of unadulterated male beefcake oozing pure male sexuality—and he was holding her mother's cake in one large hand, safe and sound.

She swallowed hard against the sizzling heat radiating off of Luke Braden, one of only two men in Trusty who had ever stood up for her—and the man whose face she pictured on lonely nights. When she'd decided to come back to Trusty, her mind had immediately raced back to Luke. She'd wondered—maybe even hoped—she'd run into him. Residency had been all-consuming and exhausting, with working right through thirty-six-hour shifts. She hadn't had time to even think about dating, much less had time for actual dating. Her body tingled in places that hadn't been touched by a man in a very long time.

"I think it's okay." With smoldering dark eyes and a wickedly naughty grin, he eyed the cake.

His deep voice shuddered through her. Okay, Daisy. Get ahold of yourself. He might have saved you in high school, but that was eleven years ago. He was no longer the cute boy with long bangs that covered perpetually hungry eyes. No, Luke Braden was anything but a boy, and by the look on his face, he had no recollection of who she was, making the torch she'd carried for him all these years heavy as lead.

"Thank you." She reached for the cake, and he pulled it just out of reach as his eyes took a slow stroll down her body, which was enough to weaken her knees and wake her up. She'd left Trusty after high school and had purposely found work near her college and med school during summers and breaks, so her memory of the people she'd gone to school with was sketchy at best after eleven years, but his was a face she'd never forget.

"You've got your hands full. Why don't I carry it to your car?" His dark hair was cut short on the sides. The top was longer, thick and windblown in that sexy way that only happened in magazines. His square jaw was peppered with rough stubble, and Daisy had the urge to reach out and stroke it. His stubble, that is.

Luke looked like one of those guys who took what they wanted and left a trail of women craving more in their wake, and in high school his reputation had been just that. *Carry the cake to my car? Like that won't end up with you trying to carry me to your bed?* The idea sent another little shudder through her. It was exactly what she'd been hoping—and waiting—for.

He had been two years ahead of Daisy in school, and because she'd spent her high school years fighting a reputation she didn't deserve, she'd kept a low profile. She'd darkened her hair in medical school to combat the stereotypical harassment that went along with having blond hair, blue eyes, and a body that she took care of. Now, thanks to a six-dollar box of dye every few weeks, it was a medium shade of brown. She'd never forget the time in her sophomore year when Luke had stood up for her. She'd carried a fantasy of him thinking of her for all these years. Was I really that invisible to you? Apparently, she was, because by the look on his face, he didn't recognize her. It stung like salt in a wound.

Her eyes caught on a flash of silver on his arm. Duct tape? She squinted to be sure. Yes. The wide strip of silver on his bulging biceps was indeed duct tape, and there was blood dripping from beneath it.

He followed her gaze to his arm with a shrug. "Scraped it on some wire at my ranch."

She should take her cake and walk right out the door, but the medical professional in her took over—and the hurt woman in her refused to believe he could have forgotten her that easily. She took a step back into the diner. "Margie, can I borrow your first-aid kit?"

Luke's brows knitted together as he followed her inside. "If that's for me, I don't need it. Really."

Margie handed Daisy the first-aid kit from beneath the counter. "Here you go, sugar." She eyed the tall, dark man, and her green eyes warmed. "Luke, are you causing trouble again?"

He arched a thick, dark brow. "Hardly. I'm meeting Emily here, but I'm a little early."

"Good, because the last thing you need is more trouble." Margie gave him a stern look as she came around the counter, and he flashed a warm smile, the kind a person reserved for those he cared about.

Daisy felt a stab of jealousy and quickly chided herself for it. She'd been back in town for only two weeks, and she had kept as far away from gossip as she could, but she couldn't help wondering what type of trouble Luke had gotten into. Her life was crazy enough without a guy in it. Especially a guy with enticing eyes and a sexy smile who deserved the reputation she didn't. She focused on his arm and slipped into doctor mode, which she was, thankfully, very good at. In doctor mode she could separate the injured patient from the hot guy.

Luke shot a look at Daisy, then back to Margie. "Can't believe everything you hear."

I bet.

"Glad to hear that." Margie touched his arm like she might her son. "I have to help the customers, but it's good to see you, Luke."

He flashed that killer smile again, then shifted his eyes back to Daisy, who was armed and ready with antiseptic. "I don't allow strangers to undress my wounds." He held out a hand. "Luke."

"You really don't remember me." Even though she'd seen it in his eyes, it still burned. "Daisy Honey?"

His sexy smile morphed into an amused one, and that amusement reached his eyes. "Was that Daisy, honey, or Daisy Honey, as in your full name?"

She bit back the ache of reality that he didn't even remember her name and passed it off with an eye roll. She turned his arm so she could inspect his duct-tape bandage. "Daisy Honey, as in my given name."

He laughed at that, a deep, hearty, friendly laugh.

She ripped the tape off fast, exposing a nasty gash in his upper arm.

"Hey." He wrenched his arm away. "With a name like Daisy Honey, I thought you'd be sweet."

She blinked several times, and in her sweetest voice, she said, "With a name like Luke Braden, I thought you'd be more manly." Shit. I can't believe I said that.

"Ouch. You don't mince words, do you?" He rubbed his arm. "I was kidding. I know who you are. I get my hay from your dad. I just didn't recognize you. The last time I saw you, your hair was blond." He ran his eyes down her body again, and damn if it didn't make her hot all over. "And you sure as hell didn't look like that."

You do remember me! She ignored Luke's comment about her looks, secretly tucking it away with delight, and went to work cleaning his cut. "How'd you do this, anyway?" She felt his eyes on her as she swabbed the dried blood from his skin.

"I was walking past a fence and didn't see the wire sticking out. Tore right through my shirt." He rolled down the edge of his torn sleeve just above his cut.

"Barbed wire, like your tattoo?" Your hot, sexy, badass

tattoo that wraps around your incredibly hard muscle?

He eyed his tattoo with a half-cocked smile. "Regular fence wire."

"Was it rusty?" She tried to ignore the heat of his assessing gaze.

He shrugged again, which seemed to be a common answer for him.

"When was your last tetanus shot?" She finished cleaning the cut and placed a fresh bandage over it before wrapping the dirty swabs in a napkin.

He shrugged. "I'm fine."

"You won't be if you get tetanus. You should stop by the medical clinic for a shot. Any of the nurses can administer it for you." She tucked her hair behind her ear and checked the time. She was definitely late, and he was definitely checking her out. Her stomach did a little flip.

"Are you a nurse?" He rolled up his torn sleeve again.

"Doctor, actually," she said with pride. She wondered if seeing her helping him stirred the memory of when he stood up for her all those years ago. By the look in his eyes, she doubted it. He had that first-meeting look, the one that read, I wonder if I have a shot, rather than the look of, You're that girl everyone said was a slut.

He nodded, and his eyes turned serious. "Well, thank you, Dr. Daisy Honey. I appreciate the care and attention you've given to my flesh."

He said *my flesh* with a sensual and evocative tone that tripped her up. She opened her mouth to respond and no words came.

Margie returned to the counter. "Can I get you something, Luke?"

Thankful for the distraction, Daisy pushed the first-aid kit across the counter, then gathered her things. "Thanks, Margie."

"I'd love coffee and two eggs over easy with toast," Luke said.

Daisy felt his eyes on her as she struggled to handle the cake, bag, and coffee again.

"Coming right up, sugar." Margie disappeared into the kitchen, and Daisy headed for the door.

He touched her arm and batted his long, dark lashes. "You're just going to dress my wound and leave? I feel so cheap."

Despite herself, she had to laugh. "That was actually kind of cute."

He narrowed his eyes, and it about stole her breath. "Cute? Not at all what I was going for."

Then you hit your mark, because it wasn't cute that's making my pulse race.

He held the door open for her. "I hope to see you around,

Daisy, honey."

"Tetanus isn't fun. You should get the shot." She forced her legs to carry her away from his heated gaze.

To continue reading, buy

TAKEN BY LOVE (FREE at the time of this publication)

More Books by Melissa

LOVE IN BLOOM SERIES

SNOW SISTERS
Sisters in Love
Sisters in Bloom
Sisters in White

THE BRADENS at Weston
Lovers at Heart
Destined for Love
Friendship on Fire
Sea of Love
Bursting with Love
Hearts at Play

THE BRADENS at Trusty
Taken by Love
Fated for Love
Romancing My Love
Flirting with Love
Dreaming of Love
Crashing into Love

THE BRADENS at Peaceful Harbor
Healed by Love
Surrender My Love
River of Love
Crushing on Love
Whisper of Love
Thrill of Love

THE BRADENS & MONTGOMERYS at Pleasant Hill – Oak Falls
Embracing Her Heart
Anything For Love
Trails of Love

THE BRADEN NOVELLAS
Promise My Love
Our New Love
Daring Her Love
Story of Love
Love at Last

THE REMINGTONS
Game of Love
Stroke of Love
Flames of Love
Slope of Love
Read, Write, Love
Touched by Love

SEASIDE SUMMERS
Seaside Dreams
Seaside Hearts
Seaside Sunsets
Seaside Secrets
Seaside Nights
Seaside Embrace
Seaside Lovers
Seaside Whispers

BAYSIDE SUMMERS
Bayside Desires
Bayside Passions
Bayside Heat
Bayside Escape

THE RYDERS
Seized by Love
Claimed by Love
Chased by Love
Rescued by Love
Swept Into Love

SEXY STANDALONE ROMANCE
Tru Blue
Truly, Madly, Whiskey
Driving Whiskey Wild
Wicked Whiskey Love

BILLIONAIRES AFTER DARK SERIES

WILD BOYS AFTER DARK
Logan
Heath
Jackson
Cooper

BAD BOYS AFTER DARK
Mick
Dylan
Carson
Brett

HARBORSIDE NIGHTS SERIES
Includes characters from the Love in Bloom series
Catching Cassidy
Discovering Delilah
Tempting Tristan

More Books by Melissa
Chasing Amanda (mystery/suspense)
Come Back to Me (mystery/suspense)
Have No Shame (historical fiction/romance)
Love, Lies & Mystery (3-book bundle)
Megan's Way (literary fiction)
Traces of Kara (psychological thriller)
Where Petals Fall (suspense)

Meet Melissa

www.MelissaFoster.com

Melissa Foster is a New York Times and USA Today bestselling and award-winning author. Her books have been recommended by USA Today's book blog, Hagerstown magazine, The Patriot, and several other print venues. Melissa has painted and donated several murals to the Hospital for Sick Children in Washington, DC.

Melissa also writes sweet romance under the pen name Addison Cole.

Visit Melissa on her website or chat with her on social media. Melissa enjoys discussing her books with book clubs and reader groups and welcomes an invitation to your event.

www.MelissaFoster.com
www.MelissaFoster.com/Newsletter
www.MelissaFoster.com/Reader-Goodies

Made in the USA
Monee, IL
10 March 2020

22988287R00062